Dear Parent:

Congratulations! Your child is taking the first steps on an exciting journey. The destination? Independent reading!

STEP INTO READING® will help your child get there. The program offers five steps to reading success. Each step includes fun stories and colorful art. There are also Step into Reading Sticker Books, Step into Reading Math Readers, Step into Reading Phonics Readers, Step into Reading Write-In Readers, and Step into Reading Phonics Boxed Sets—a complete literacy program with something for every child.

Learning to Read, Step by Step!

Ready to Read   Preschool–Kindergarten
• big type and easy words • rhyme and rhythm • picture clues
For children who know the alphabet and are eager to begin reading.

Reading with Help   Preschool–Grade 1
• basic vocabulary • short sentences • simple stories
For children who recognize familiar words and sound out new words with help.

Reading on Your Own   Grades 1–3
• engaging characters • easy-to-follow plots • popular topics
For children who are ready to read on their own.

Reading Paragraphs   Grades 2–3
• challenging vocabulary • short paragraphs • exciting stories
For newly independent readers who read simple sentences with confidence.

Ready for Chapters   Grades 2–4
• chapters • longer paragraphs • full-color art
For children who want to take the plunge into chapter books but still like colorful pictures.

STEP INTO READING® is designed to give every child a successful reading experience. The grade levels are only guides. Children can progress through the steps at their own speed, developing confidence in their reading, no matter what their grade.

Remember, a lifetime love of reading starts with a single step!

For Leo and Ramona —A.J.

Step into Reading, Random House, and the Random House colophon are registered trademarks of Random House, Inc.

Visit us on the Web!
StepIntoReading.com
randomhousé.com/kids

Educators and librarians, for a variety of teaching tools, visit us at
RHTeachersLibrarians.com

ISBN: 978-0-7364-2978-8 (trade) — ISBN: 978-0-7364-8125-0 (lib. bdg.)

Printed in the United States of America   10 9 8 7 6 5 4 3 2 1

Fast Kart, Slow Kart

By Apple Jordan

Illustrated by the Disney Storybook Artists

Random House 🏠 New York

This is Ralph.

Ralph <u>wrecks</u> things.

This is Felix.

Felix <u>fixes</u> things.

Ralph and Felix live
in a video game.
When the game ends,
Felix is up <u>high</u>.

Ralph is down <u>low</u>.

Felix is <u>clean</u>.

Ralph is <u>dirty</u>.

A girl is
outside the game.

Felix and his friends
are <u>inside</u> the game.

Ralph climbs <u>up</u>.

Ralph falls <u>down</u>.

Vanellope is <u>small</u>.

Ralph is <u>big</u>.

Ralph is <u>tall</u>.

Vanellope is <u>short</u>.

Vanellope is <u>happy</u>.

Vanellope is <u>sad</u>.

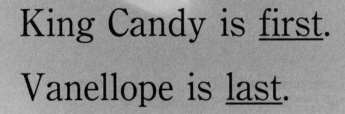

King Candy is <u>first</u>.

Vanellope is <u>last</u>.

Now Vanellope
is in <u>front</u> . . .
and in <u>back</u>!

Vanellope goes <u>fast</u>.

Vanellope goes <u>slow</u>.

Vanellope wins!